A Remarkable Eye

JEAN-PAUL FERRERO

A Remarkable Eye

The Australian Photographs
of Jean-Paul Ferrero

VIKING

The Australian Photographs of Jean-Paul Ferrero

'I have known Jean-Paul since he settled in Australia almost twenty years ago. In the intervening period, he surpassed most Australians in his knowledge and appreciation for this country. His passion for photography was immense and his hunger for new horizons persisted to the very end.'

Mike Gillam, photographer and friend,
Alice Springs, September 2000

Through his photographs, French-born Jean-Paul Ferrero offered new ways of visualising the Australian landscape and its wildlife. This book is at once a celebration of Australia and a tribute to a photographer whose untimely death has left us wondering what new insights might have followed.

At the age of 50, after only 20 years of photographing Australia, Jean-Paul Ferrero died of pancreatic cancer. Yet within that relatively short space of time, he amassed a formidable body of work, the best examples of which will continue to challenge popular perceptions of this continent for many years to come. In his quest to engage and excite the viewer, Ferrero gently pushed the boundaries of commercial photography and encouraged his clients to present Australia in new ways.

While so many of his photographs are breathtakingly beautiful, Ferrero thought of himself as a communicator rather than an artist. Books and magazines – not art galleries – were his preferred forums. As wildlife filmmaker David Parer explains in his tribute to Ferrero, he was essentially a storyteller, forever working with his audience in mind. Over time, Ferrero came to see a new dimension to his role as communicator. To quote author and photographer Reg Morrison, 'As environmental storm clouds began to gather round this hard-pressed, overpopulated planet, Jean-Paul's role as umbilical link between the real world and the fantasy world of the city dweller became a crucial one indeed'.

In recent years, Ferrero had tentative thoughts of publishing a collection of his Australian photographs – a combination of wildlife, aerial and landscape images. This was an idea he raised with some of his closest friends and colleagues, but never actively pursued. As this publication attests, there was no shortage of fine material to work with. In order to narrow down the selection, exacting criteria had to be set: an image would only be included if it had the power to intrigue, surprise, thrill or move the viewer in some way. It is a credit to Ferrero's talents that the task of reducing the number of photographs was so difficult.

Previous page
First rays of light, Purnululu National Park, Western Australia, June 2000

Jean-Marc La Roque, photographer and friend, recalls: 'Jean-Paul was so frail at this stage that he could only work early morning and evening, resting during the day. After much discussion, we settled on this location the night before. We left camp at 4 a.m. to set up our equipment and wait for the sun. Jean-Paul, who always liked to fill his images, set up to take full advantage of the foreground, while I concentrated on the range in the background. As the first light slowly appeared, I could see in his eyes the intense pleasure he felt of being here, watching and recording the details of the landscape as they emerged.'

One of the extraordinary things about Ferrero's images, something that this selection serves to highlight, is the blurring of distinctions between photographic genres – wildlife, aerial and landscape photography blend almost seamlessly on these pages. His most striking images are arguably those that give a new perspective to a familiar subject: migrating whales viewed from the air, oblique aerials that defy traditional notions of a flat and barren interior, and dynamic photographs of animals within the landscape.

Such images are the product of a photographer who completely mastered a wide range of equipment and techniques. Ferrero switched effortlessly from one camera or lens to another in response to the particular demands of his subject matter. This mastery extended to the darkroom where he spent just as much time developing and perfecting his images.

Jean-Paul Ferrero photographing an olive python. December 1999 (Greg Miles)

Technical excellence was matched by an instinct for what Ansel Adams famously called 'visualization'. Part of the creative process can be practised and learned, Adams said, but beyond that lies 'the domain of personal vision and insight, the creative "eye" of the individual'. This collection of images highlights Ferrero's talent for seeing and representing the extraordinary coincidences, patterns and compositions of nature.

Ferrero's Australian legacy is substantial and twofold. He left behind an outstanding body of work that continues to represent Australia in books and magazines around the world. He also recognised and nurtured the talents of others through his Sydney-based photo library, Auscape International. Meanwhile, he continued to travel abroad, returning with breakthrough wildlife portfolios, including a series on the kagu of New Caledonia, the proboscis monkey of Borneo and the chinstrap penguin of the Antarctic.

It might be said that Ferrero's international perspective gave a certain edge to his Australian work. As the distinguished Californian based wildlife photographer Frans Lanting explains in the following tribute, Ferrero's images served to modernise our perception of Australian wildlife and the landscape it inhabits. This book is a modest record of Jean-Paul's Australian image-making and a celebration of his remarkable eye for nature.

The unmistakable imprint

As a wildlife filmmaker who shared Jean-Paul's passion for wild animals and wild places, I welcome this volume of his Australian pictures.

I knew of Jean-Paul Ferrero through his photographs many years prior to meeting him. His startling images of the Australian landscape and action-packed pictures of the unique animals that inhabit our island continent adorned many books and magazines from the 1970s onwards – long before Australia's fauna was widely celebrated.

In particular, I remember the large and lavishly illustrated book, *The Kangaroo,* by Michael Archer. All the impressive and eye-catching images in this volume bore the unmistakable imprint of a Ferrero photo – wild animals in their environment, alert, living on the edge, yet resplendent against the backdrop of the Australian bush. His pictures always have energy, vitality, impact and of course technical perfection. They inform, they amuse, they educate and, more importantly, they involve at an emotional level.

Jean-Paul always wanted to do more than just create individual stunning images. In his own work and through Auscape International, his photo agency, he sought to compile groups of photographs that created a complete feeling for the animal in its environment. Because of my background in filmmaking, I understood this approach. Jean-Paul was a grand storyteller – with an eye for the unusual and the imagination to put together a selection of pictures whose sum was greater than the parts. To me these were the most important features of Jean-Paul's genius.

Searching for words to describe Jean-Paul's approach and his passion for wildlife and wilderness photography, I come up with the following, somewhat inadequate selection: creative, obsessive, demanding, critical, honest, intuitive, uncompromising and forever after a new angle.

Jean-Paul was always pushing the limits – exploring the new, the unusual, the unknown. Or working old subjects in a new way. Technically, he continually pushed back frontiers – using a gyro-stabiliser to photograph Australia from the air – a five-year odyssey that took him in a light plane to every corner of our continent. He used tilt lenses for 35mm cameras so as to give a three-dimensional look to the two-dimensional form of a photograph. And he encouraged the use of multiple flash techniques to capture the texture, colour, action and behaviour of our wildlife, while minimising the effects of artificial light.

For us who knew and loved him and respected his bountiful talents, he is greatly missed. But his courage, his inspiration and his remarkable images will live on.

David Parer, wildlife photographer and filmmaker

Behind the camera

In 1991 I met Jean-Paul Ferrero in northern Borneo. I was there with my wife and partner, Christine Eckstrom, to photograph a cross-section of Borneo's natural history for *National Geographic*. Jean-Paul was by himself for the difficult task of photographing proboscis monkeys. Our paths crossed along the Kinabatangan River where we both floated in small boats through tidal creeks looking for those rare moments when a proboscis monkey was briefly visible enough for a photograph. Chris and I left after a few days to pursue other subjects; Jean-Paul stayed on for more than a month, living and working under primitive conditions determined to do something no other photographer had done yet. And he did. I was just as impressed by his attitude of cheerful optimism in the face of adversity as I was by the quality of the proboscis photographs I saw in print later on.

In the years since, I had the pleasure to get to know Jean-Paul better, both professionally and personally. He combined a passion for natural history with superb photographic talents and applied both skills to create a memorable body of work. He helped modernise our perception of Australia's natural history wonders by tackling one challenging subject after another with creative ingenuity, raising standards for everybody else.

Jean-Paul was a pioneer who broke new ground covering his part of the world – Australia, Papua New Guinea and parts of Indonesia and Oceania. With his photo essay about New Caledonia's kagu, a rare and secretive forest bird, he took his photographic mastery to a new level of virtuosity and created a species record that will endure for a long time. But Jean-Paul's talents went far beyond making photographs. Not satisfied with the existing situation for photographic representation, he founded his own stock agency, Auscape International, and grew it into a prime collection of Australian natural history images, showcasing not just his own work, but that of other talented photographers as well.

Every great photographer's images reflect the person behind the camera as much as the subject in front of it. And that is true of Jean-Paul. He was a man of great taste, which he applied to gourmet cooking as well as to his photographic compositions. He possessed a *joie de vivre* which infused both his personal relationships and his photographs with a flair that made everything seem self-evident and natural. As a friend we miss his presence dearly, but as a photographer he will remain with us. Through his images Jean-Paul immortalised his own spirit and the natural world he celebrated in his life.

Frans Lanting, nature photographer

Endangered kagu. endemic to New Caledonia

'Photographs are magic.
I'm crazy about pictures.'
Jean-Paul Ferrero

Need a friend? Join the cubs

IN the normal run of things, when a badger meets a fox they give each other the widest of berths.

But when you're tiny, helpless and all alone in the world, you need all the friends you can get.

These two orphans were introduced at the Wildlife Aid Centre in Leatherhead, Surrey, and rapidly became inseparable.

Beth the baby badger and Willow the fox cub, both of which were abandoned by their parents, are thriving thanks to the loving care of centre founders Simon and Jill Cowell, who are helped by more than 70 volunteers.

Jill said that Beth, found in a ditch near Box Hill, Surrey, was the first baby badger in three years to be brought in. 'It's very rare for a cub to leave the sett.'

The centre relies on donations to survive and the helpline number is 0839 800132.

Picture: MIKE HOLLIST

BRITISH MODELS LEFT STANDING IN SATISFACTION ROAD TEST

TOP of the survey: The Toyota Corolla, left, was said to have the fewest problems of any car in Britain

BOTTOM: The Vauxhall Frontera, right, was said to be 'a notably poor performer in its first year, beset by all sorts of niggling problems'

Japan's easy riders

Toyota and Mazda take honours in drivers' poll

By MICHAEL KEMP, Motoring Correspondent

JAPANESE cars have taken eight out of the top ten places in a survey among British motorists.

The remaining places, judged on reliability, customer satisfaction and manufacturer's care, were filled by Germany and Malaysia.

The best British model was the Rover 200 — lagging ten points behind the top car, the Japanese Toyota

In a six-page questionnaire taking on average 30 minutes to complete, the drivers were asked what it was like to live

as the 'Bible' of reports reveal-ing customer satisfaction. JD Powers, with the help of

The second-placed Mazda 323, was said to score 'highly across all areas' And the Toyota Carina — third

with 91 points, was said to report a

also some surprising comments. For example, the JD Powers said a Czech Skoda 'will bring owners as

survey of customer satisfacti But the cost was likely to an estimated £30,000 a y from each firm — a total

THE BEST

- Toyota Corolla — 92
- Mazda 323 — 91
- Toyota Carina — 90
- Honda Accord — 89
- Honda Civic — 89

- Mazda 626 — 89
- Toyota MR2 — 89
- Mercedes 190 — 87
- Daihatsu — 86
- Proton — 86

THE WORST

- Fiat Tipo — 72
- Renault 21 — 72
- VW Golf — 72
- Ford Granada — 71
- Vauxhall Calibra — 70

- Astra & Sierra — 69
- Ford Orion — 67
- Ford Escort — 66
- Rover Mini — 63
- Vauxhall Frontera —

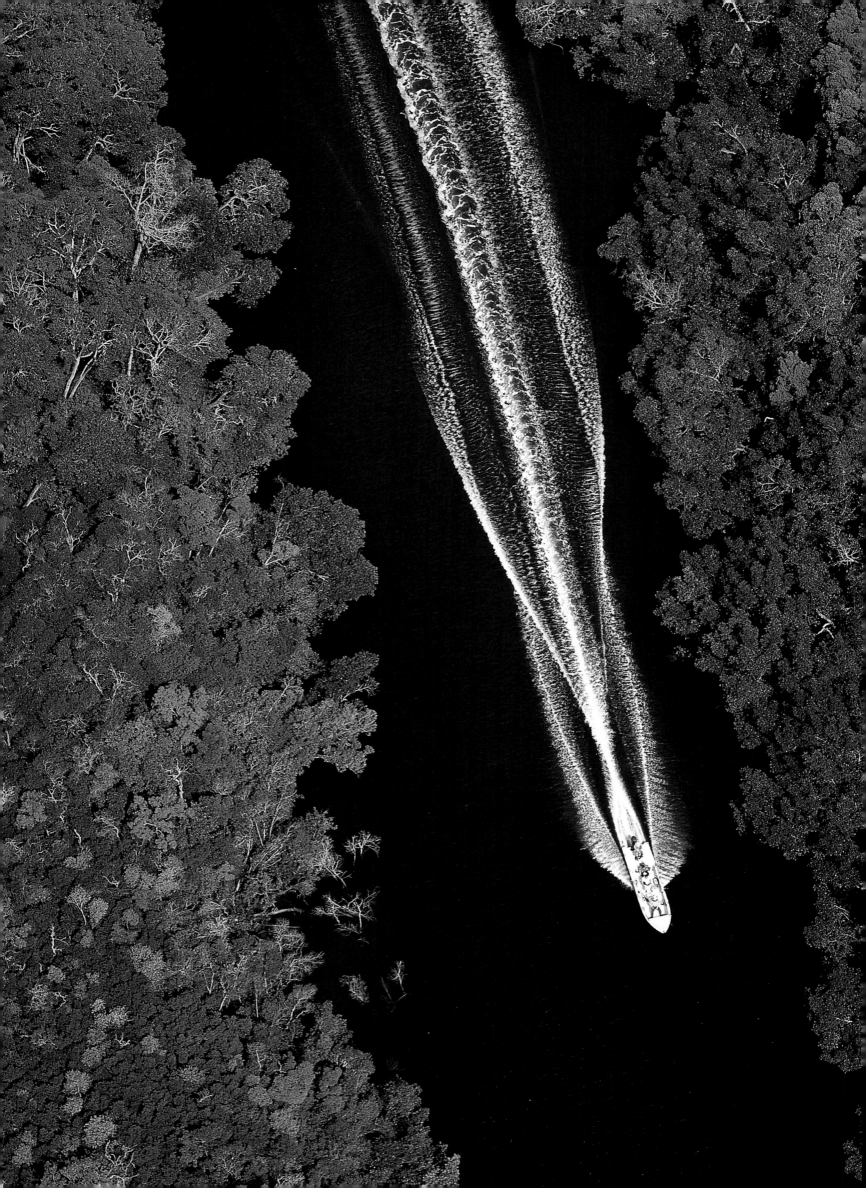

'When you take a picture, you're framing part of the world. The photographer's role is to impose his vision through his view.'

Jean-Paul Ferrero

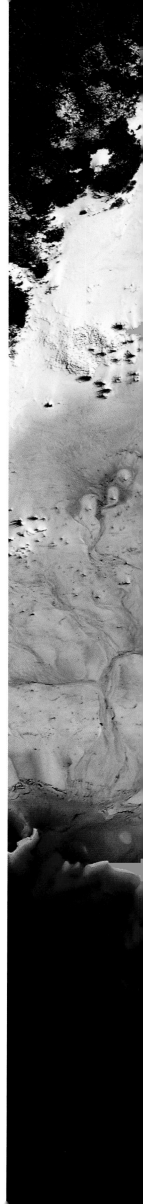

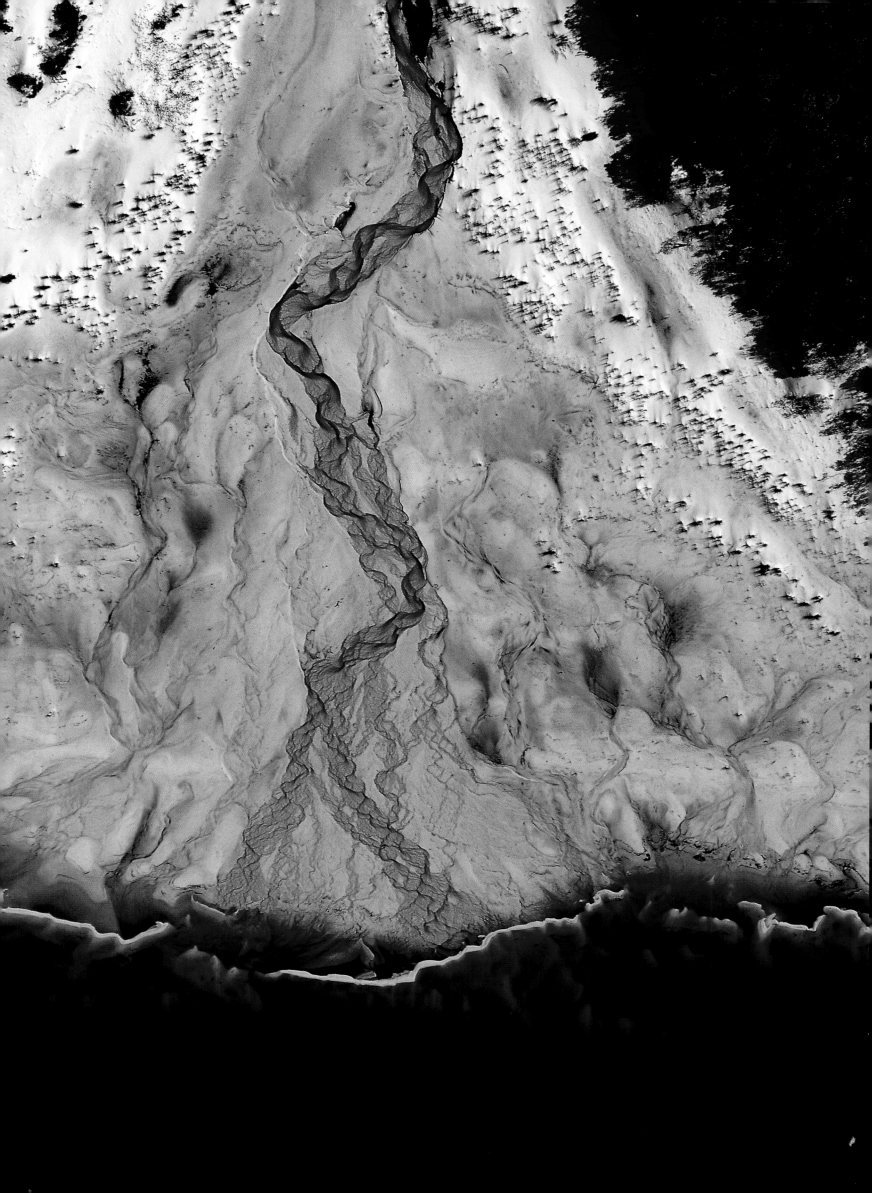

'You can spend an entire day doing nothing except waiting for the right moment.'
Jean-Paul Ferrero

'Jean-Paul's aerial photographs were carefully planned.
      He used angle and altitude to create
   magnificent foregrounds.'

Bob Mossel. pilot

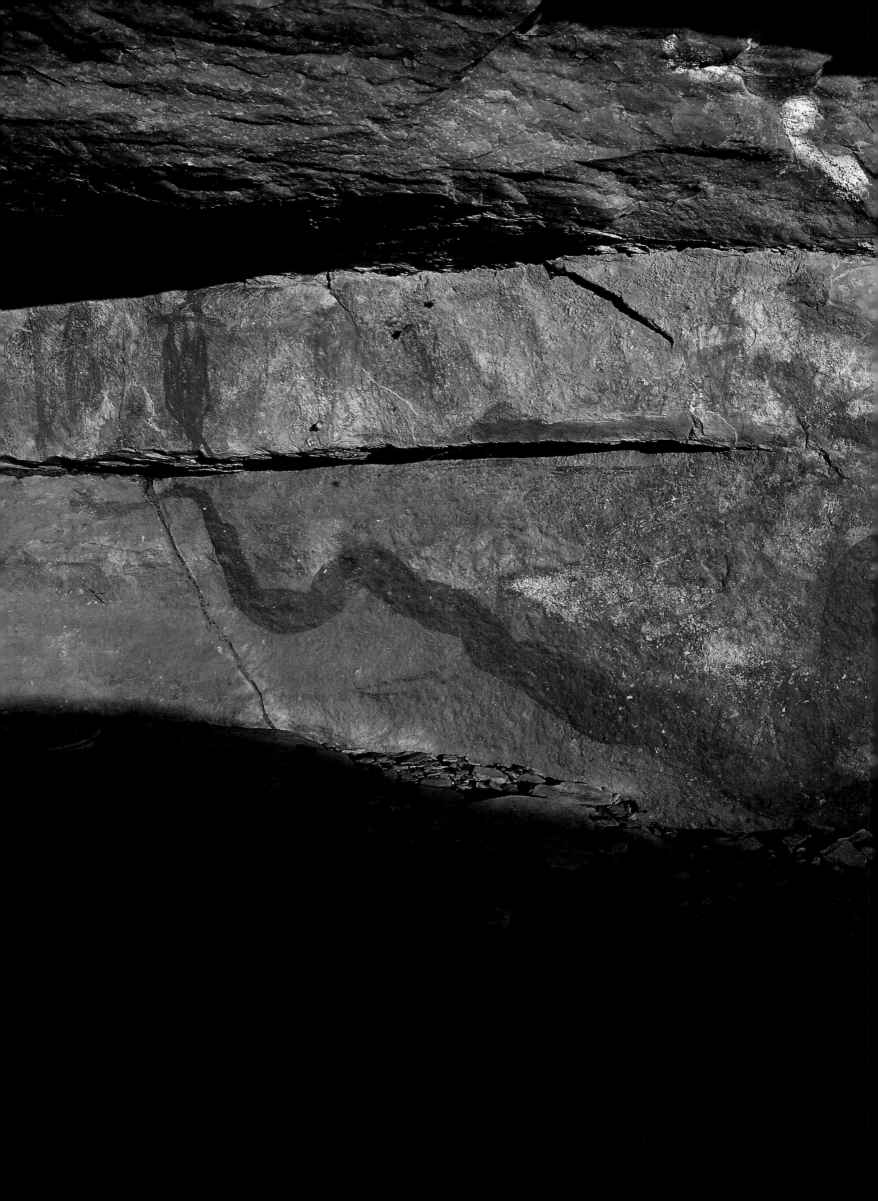

'No one sets out to become
a photographer
and then discovers wildlife;
you're into wildlife first.
Then comes the photography.' Jean-Paul Ferrero

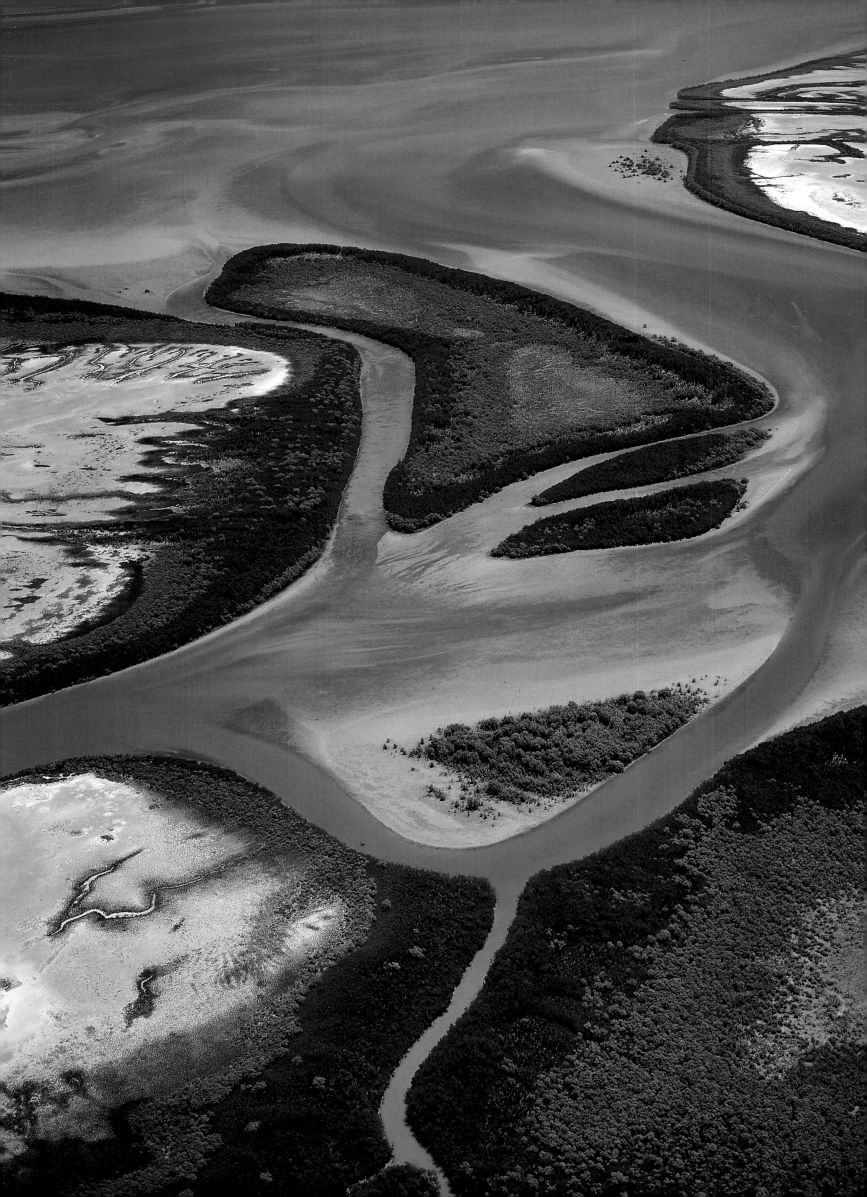

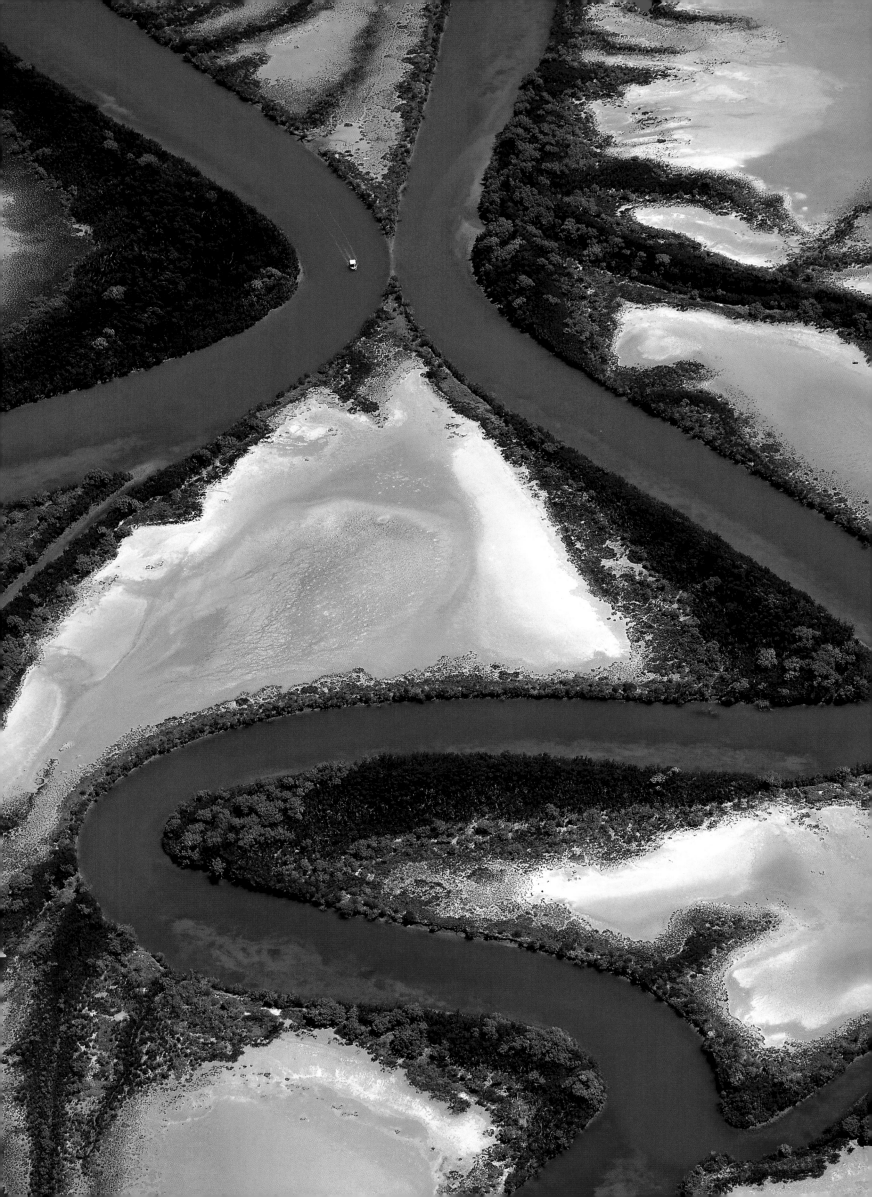

'You present in two dimensions
what exists in three,
so you have to **simplify the message** . . .
organise the chaos
of visual information.'
Jean-Paul Ferrero

'Some people say they can **recognise my pictures,** but I can't believe that . . . I think it would be difficult with this sort of photography to have a style.' Jean-Paul Ferrero

'Several genera of flowering plants, normally
　　　a minor element in the landscape, were now
　　　　　strangely dominant and the most spectacular
　　　　　　　of them peaked while we worked.

　　　　　In 25 years I have never seen such a display
　　　　　from the many species of *Ptilotus*.

　　　One evening, we drove to a remote campsite
　　　on a high plateau overlooking the Simpson Desert.

At dawn, a line of mesas materialised on the
horizon and we saw that every slope and gully
was awash with large purple *Ptilotus exaltatus*.'

Mike Gillam, travel companion
on Ferrero's last expedition

'There exist certain things I find beautiful, but because they're inexplicable, the best way to share them is to take pictures of them.'

Jean-Paul Ferrero

'We were flying quite high over the salt pans when
    all of a sudden Jean-Paul spotted a herd of camels
        running through the shallow waters of Lake Gairdner.

    He yelled "down, down" and we did several runs past
        them at a very low altitude. We could almost
            pull their tails.'

                    Bob Mossel, pilot

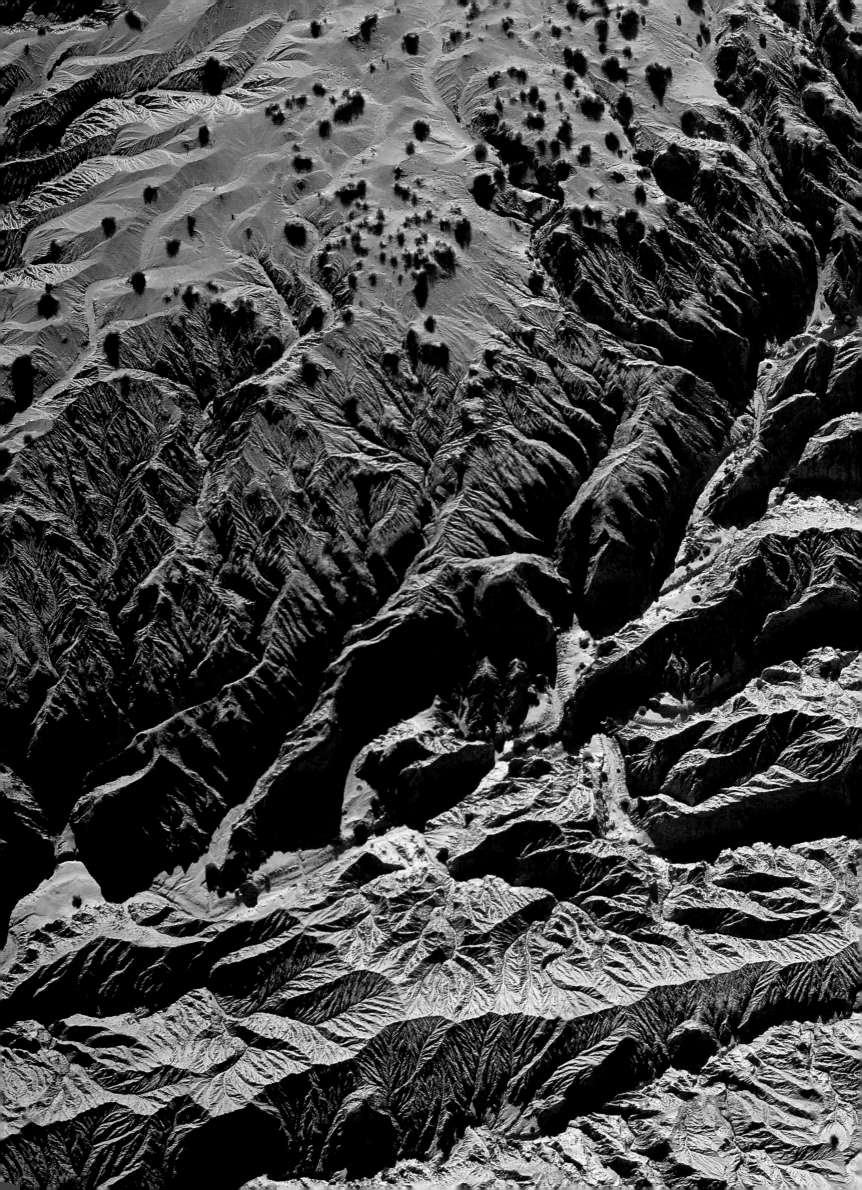

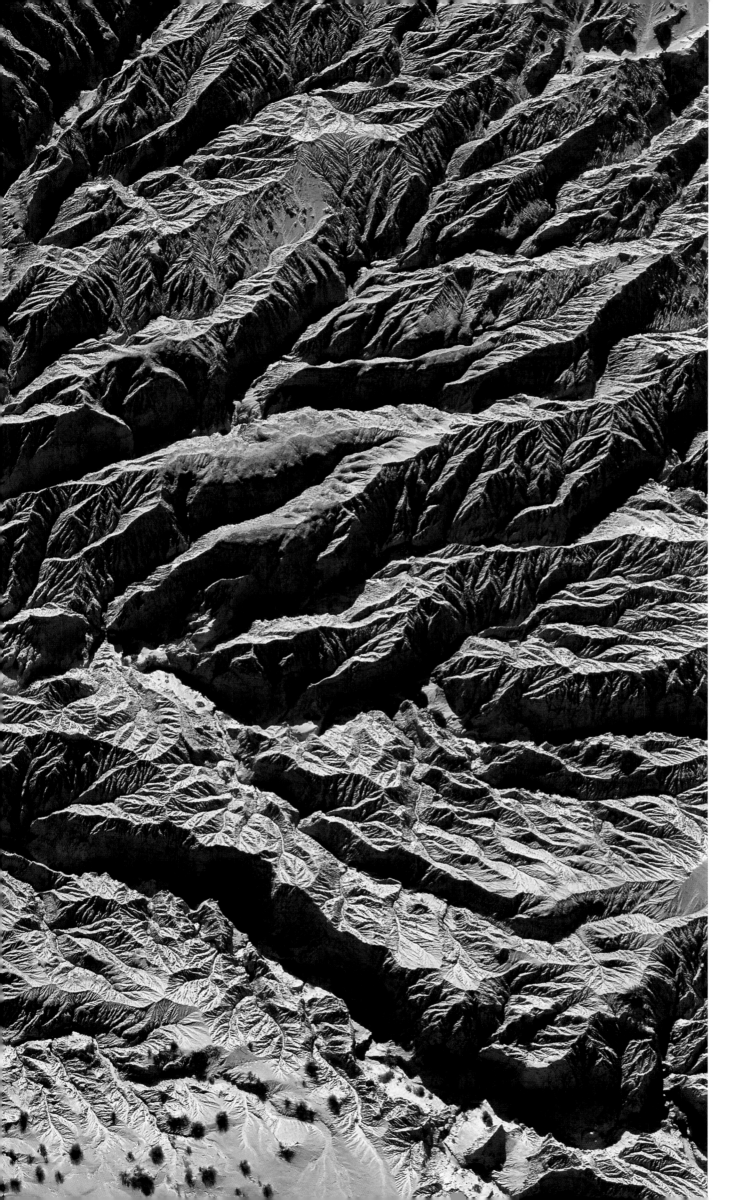

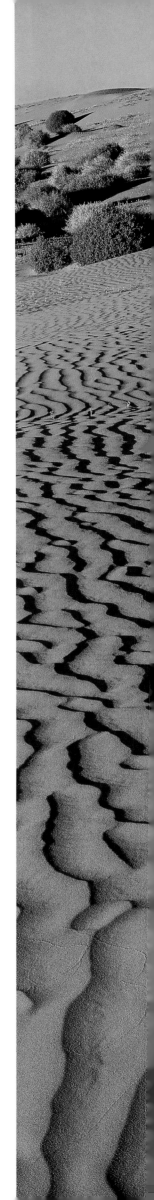

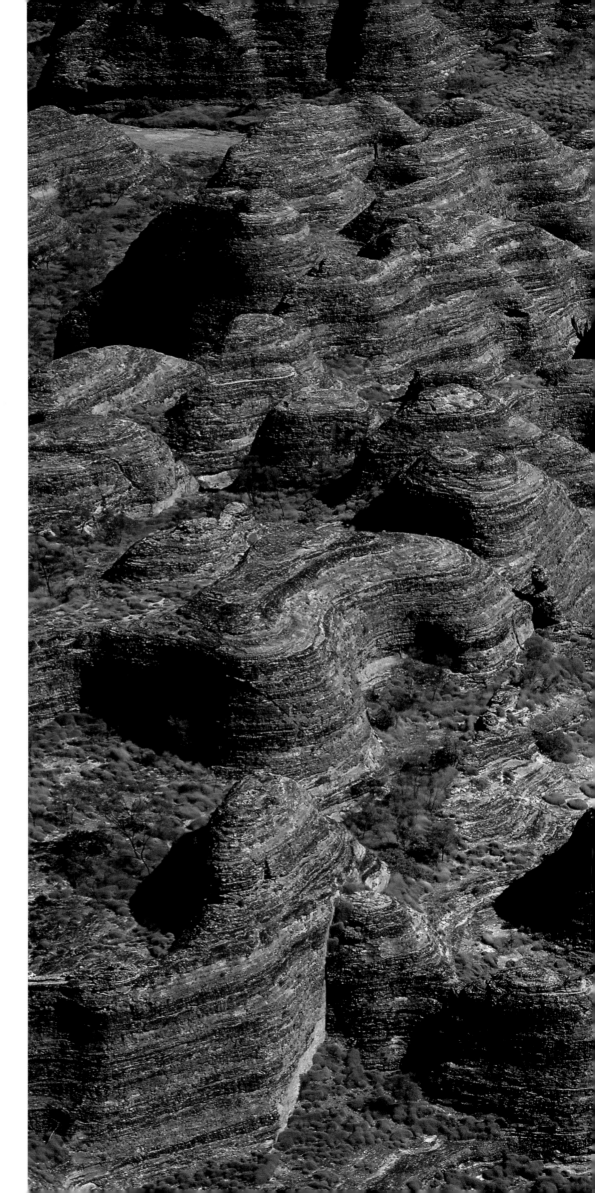

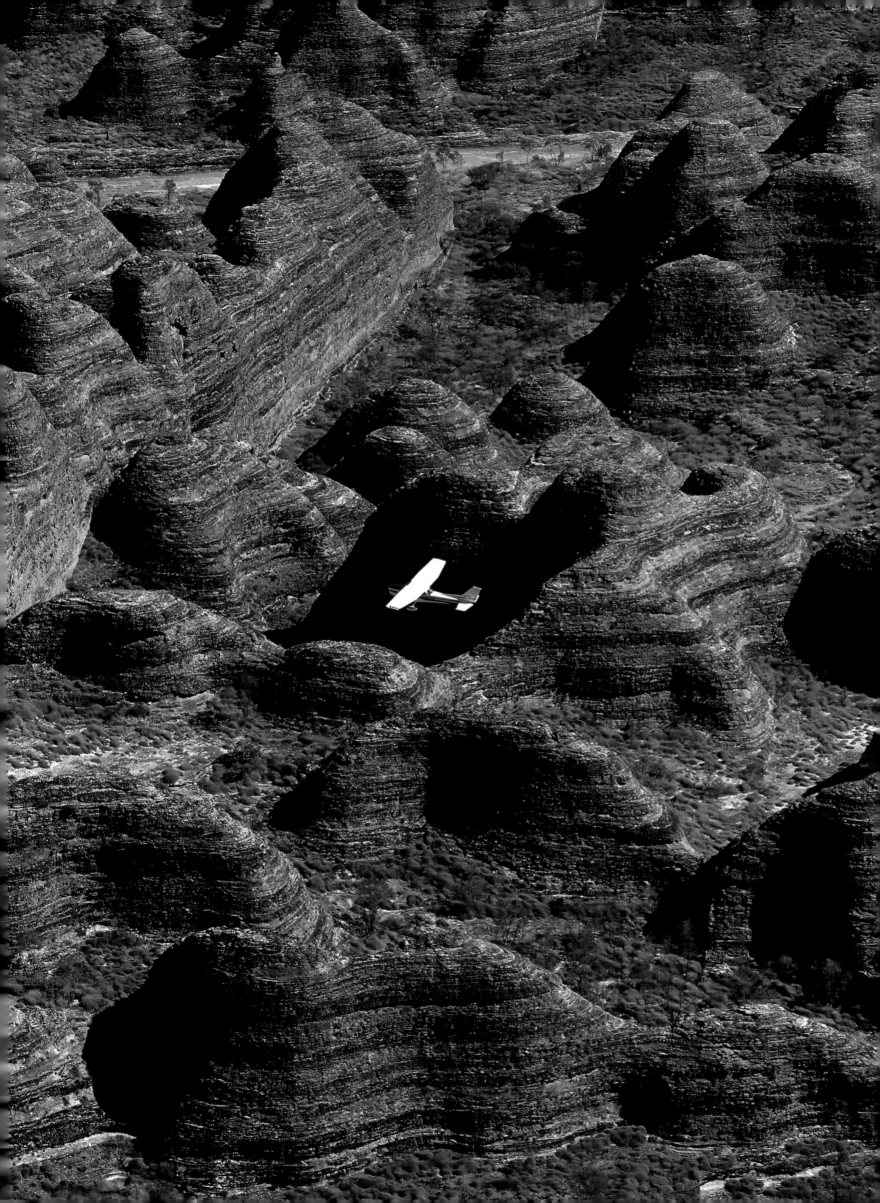

'I've never thought that
photography is an art.'
Jean-Paul Ferrero

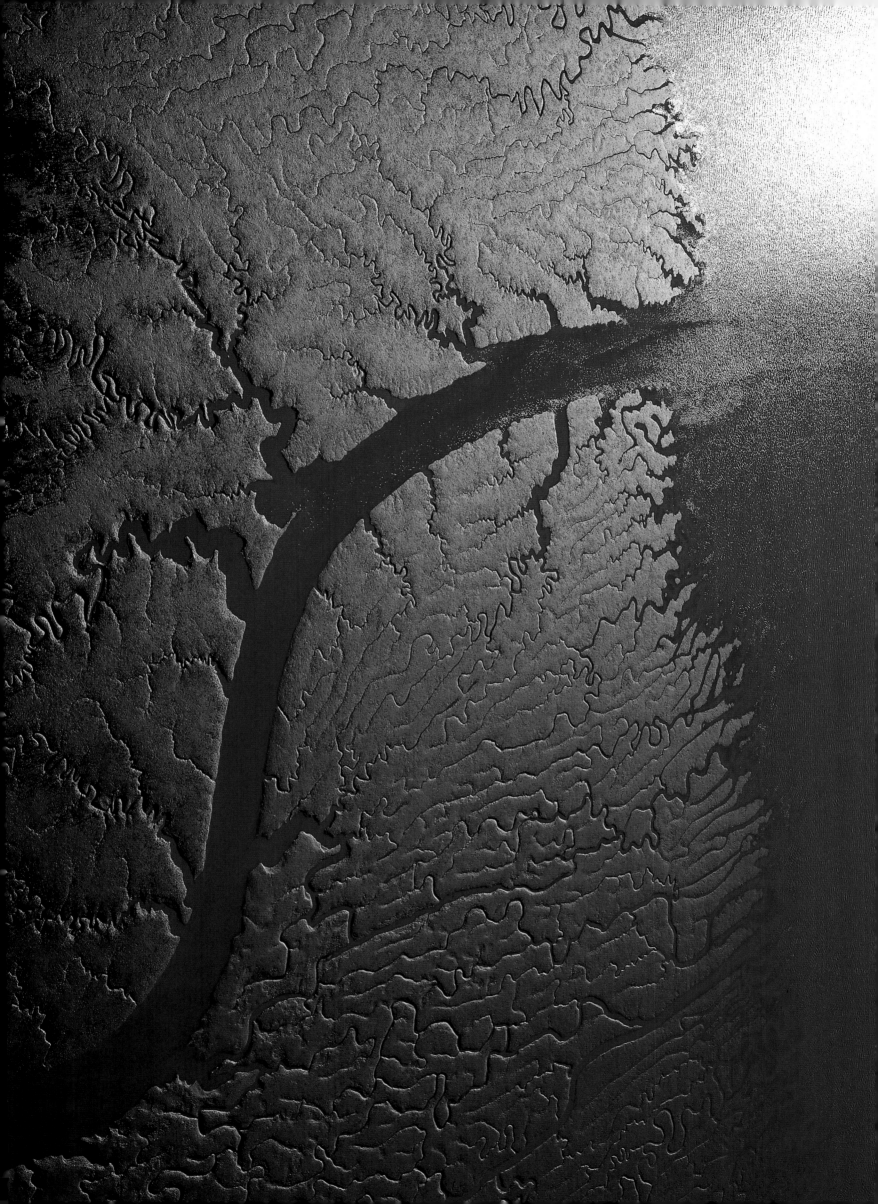

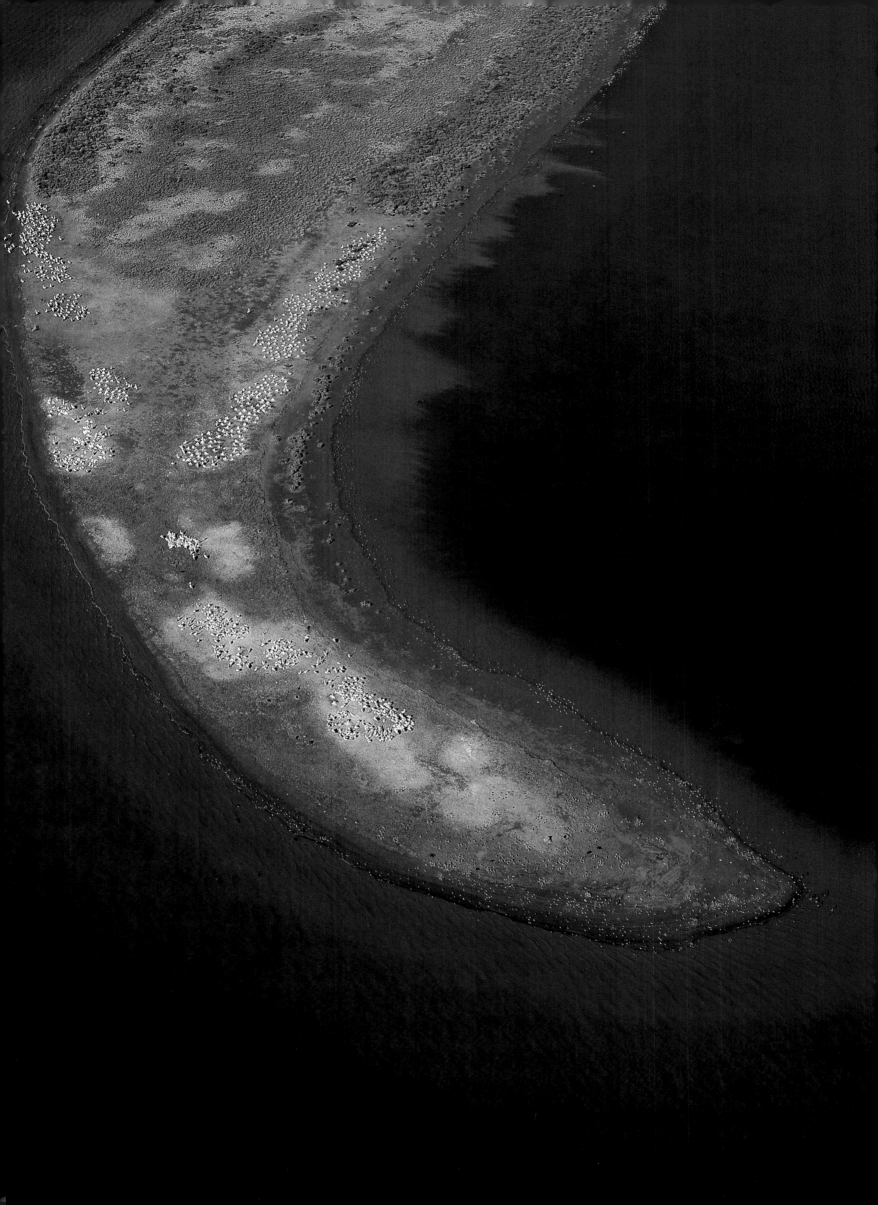

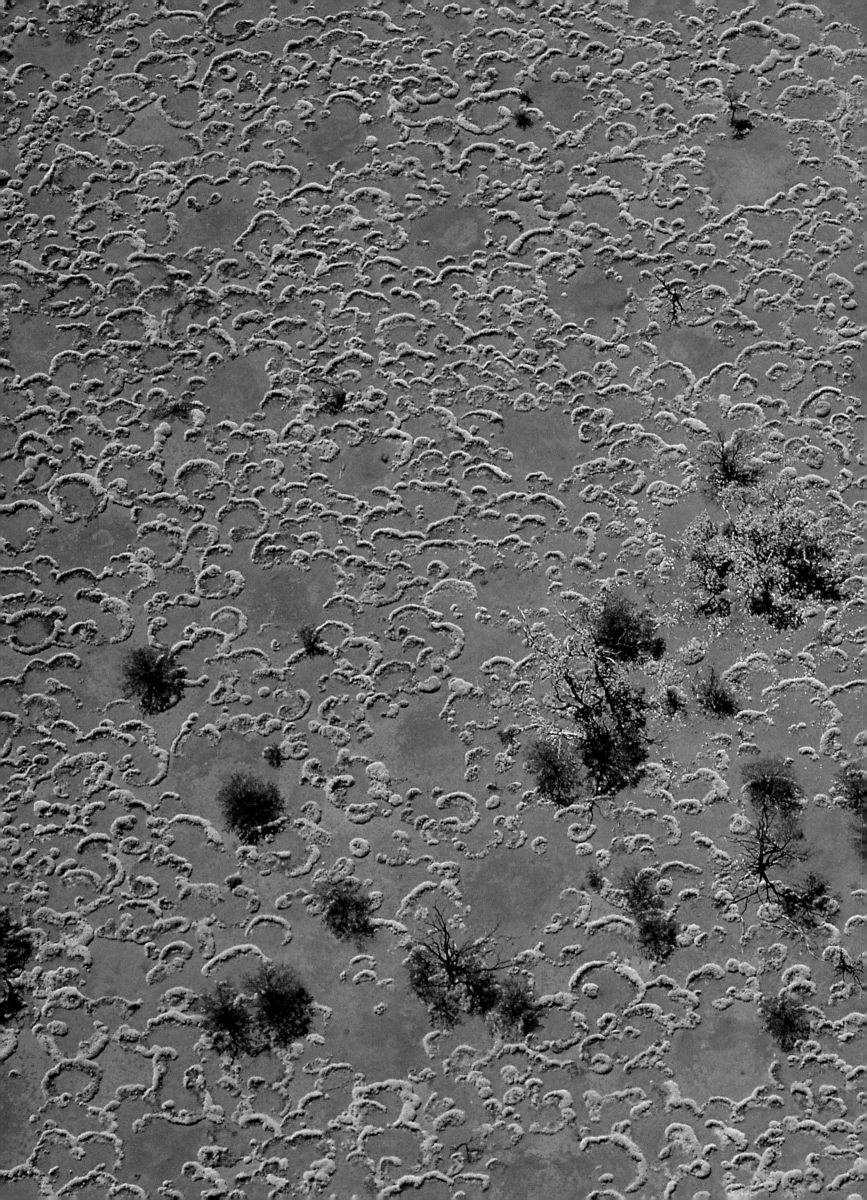

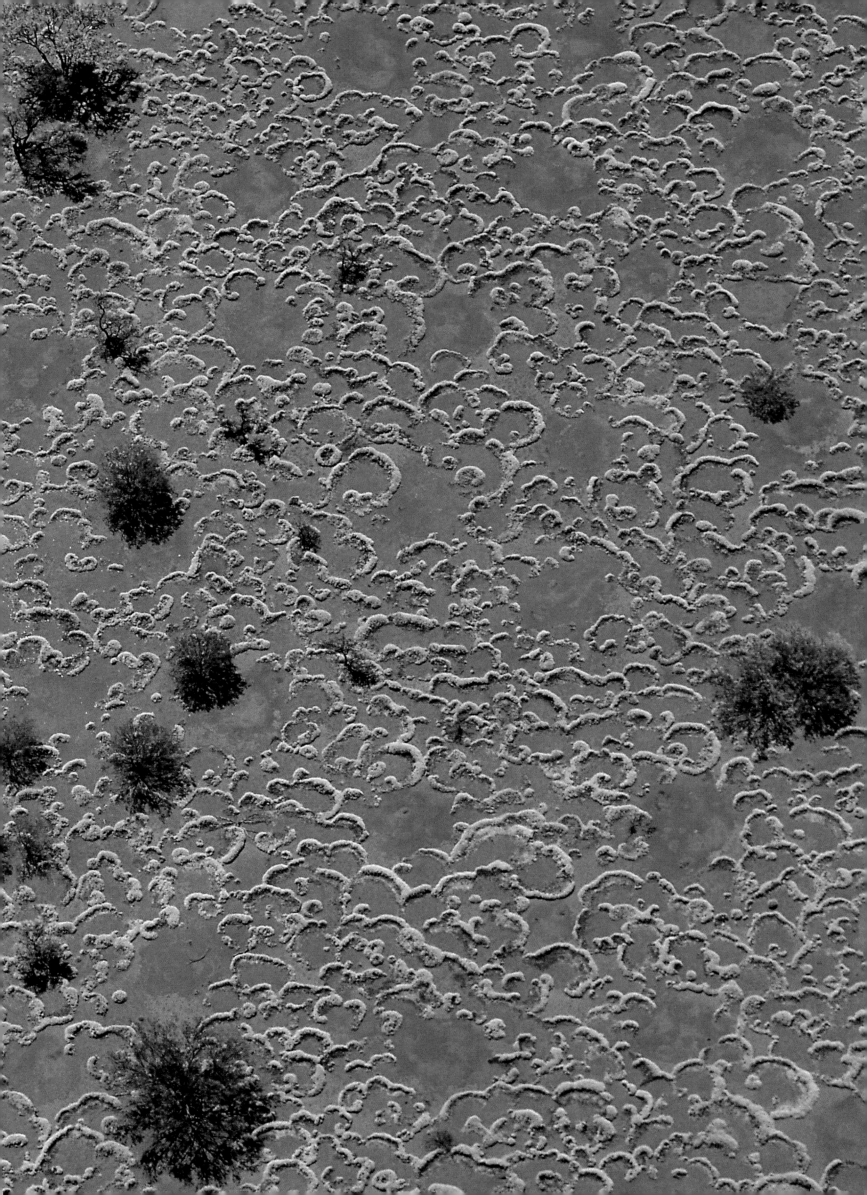

'I don't understand photographers
who only show their work in exhibitions.
For me, the best place for a picture
is in a magazine, a book.'
Jean-Paul Ferrero

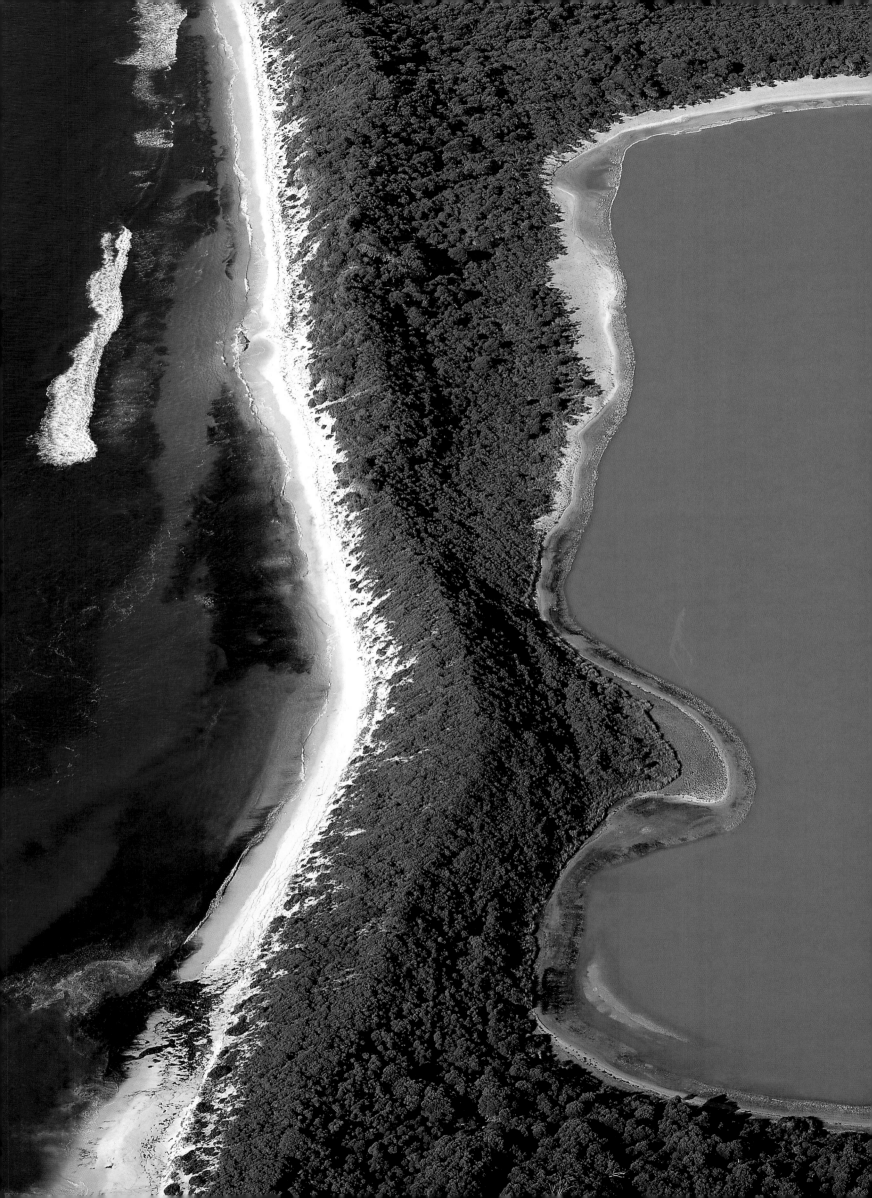

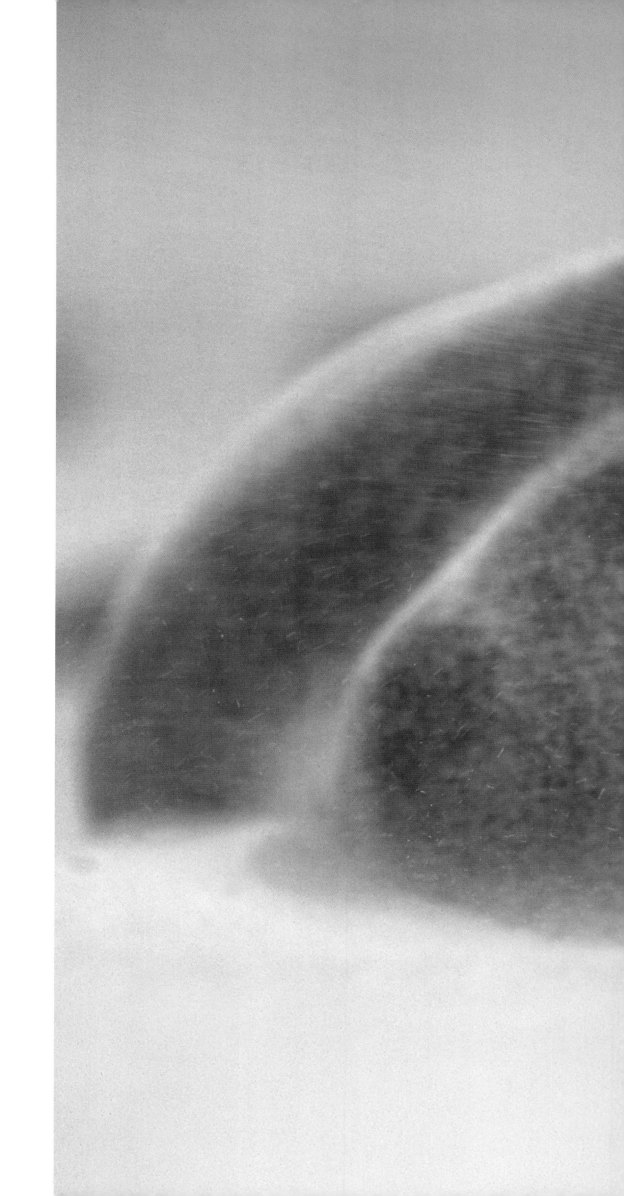

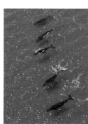
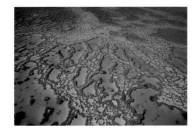

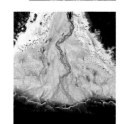

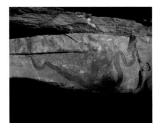

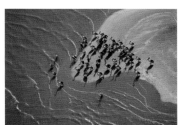

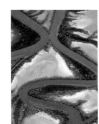

Mount Conner, flat-topped mesa,
Central Australia, Northern Territory
September 1998

page 62

Kata Tjuṯa (The Olgas) at sunset
with Uluru (Ayers Rock) in distance,
Uluru–Kata Tjuṯa National Park,
Northern Territory
September 1998

page 64

Crimson foxtail
Ptilotus atriplicifolius, with
Uluru (Ayers Rock) in distance,
Central Australia, Northern Territory
August 2000

page 67

Tall mulla mulla *Ptilotus exaltatus*,
Charlotte Range, Central Australia,
Northern Territory
August 2000

page 69

Budgerigars *Melopsittacus
undulatus*, Sturt National Park,
New South Wales
October 1996

page 70

Thorny devil *Moloch horridus*,
Gibson Desert, Western Australia
August 1988

page 72

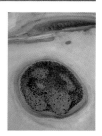

Lake Amadeus (salt lake),
Central Australia,
Northern Territory
May 1997

page 75

Salt-covered bush,
Lake Hart, South Australia
October 1988

page 77

Lake Gairdner (salt lake),
South Australia
September 1998

page 78

One-humped camels *Camelus
dromedarius* in shallow water
on Lake Gairdner (salt lake),
South Australia
September 1998

page 81

Eroded sandcliffs, Lake Eyre (North),
Lake Eyre National Park,
South Australia
May 1997

page 82

Everard Ranges, with Musgrave
Ranges in distance, South Australia
May 1997

page 84

Longitudinal sand dunes,
Strzelecki Desert, South Australia
October 1996

page 87

Strzelecki Desert, South Australia
October 1997

page 88

Red kangaroo *Macropus rufus*,
Sturt National Park,
New South Wales
February 1980

page 90

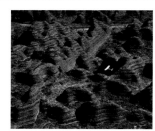

Bungle Bungle Range, near
Cathedral Gorge, Purnululu National
Park, Western Australia
May 1997

page 92

Talbot Bay islands, Kimberley
coastline, Western Australia
May 1997

page 94

Tidal flats, Kimberley coastline,
Western Australia
May 1997

page 96

St George Basin, Prince Regent
Nature Reserve, Kimberley
coastline, Western Australia
May 1997

page 99

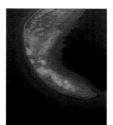

Australian pelicans *Pelecanus
conspicillatus* and black swans
Cygnus atratus, Fortescue River
floodplains, Western Australia
May 1997

page 100

Birrida (claypan), Francois Peron
National Park, Western Australia
May 1997

page 103

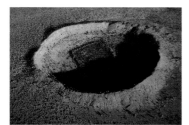

Second largest meteorite crater
in Australia, Wolfe Creek Crater
National Park, Western Australia
May 1997

page 104

Red kangaroos *Macropus rufus*,
male, female and joey, Kinchega
National Park, New South Wales
October 1996

page 107

Sand dunes and spinifex rings,
Little Sandy Desert,
Western Australia
September 1988

page 108

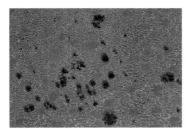

Spinifex carpet, Little Sandy Desert,
Western Australia
September 1998

page 110

Woma python *Aspidites ramsayi*,
near Alice Springs,
Northern Territory
May 1997

page 112

Cape Peron North, Francois Peron
National Park, Western Australia
May 1997

page 115

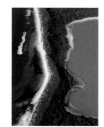

Lake Hillier, Middle Island,
Archipelago of the Recherche,
Western Australia
May 1997

page 117

New River Lagoon,
Southwest National Park, Tasmania
March 1999

page 118

Lighthouse, Tasman Island,
Tasman National Park, Tasmania
March 1999

page 121

Cushion plants, including
Dracophyllum minimum and
Abrotanella forsteroides, Walls of
Jerusalem National Park, Tasmania
February 1983

page 122

Precipitous Bluff, Southwest
National Park, Tasmania
March 1999

page 124

Australian sea lion *Neophoca
cinerea*, Seal Bay Conservation Park,
Kangaroo Island, South Australia
November 1996

page 126

Red land crabs *Gecarcoidea natalis*,
males 'dipping' to replenish water
and salt, Territory of Christmas
Island (2600 kilometres
north-west of Perth)
December 1995

page 132

'We are fortunate that photographers leave so much of themselves behind.'

Mike Gillam

Publisher's acknowledgements

The publisher would like to thank the following individuals and organisations:

Auscape International

This project would not have been possible without the support of Auscape International, the photo library established by Jean-Paul Ferrero in 1985. Despite the demands of running a busy international photo library, Vere Kenny and Sashi Kanagasabai assisted in every way to ensure that this book would be a fine tribute to their late employer and friend.

Mike Gillam, photographer

Mike Gillam, who worked alongside Ferrero in Central Australia, offered many valuable insights into his approach to image-making.

Jean-Marc La Roque, photographer

Jean-Marc La Roque's memories of working with Ferrero, and his understanding of what motivated his friend, provided an added depth to this book.

Frans Lanting, nature photographer

Acclaimed wildlife photographer Frans Lanting regularly works on assignment for *National Geographic*; his images have been featured in virtually every major magazine in the world. Lanting's photographs illustrate ten books, including *Eye to Eye* (1997), *Penguin* (1999) and *Jungles* (2000). His tribute to Ferrero appears on page ix.

Reg Morrison, author and photographer

Reg Morrison's professional respect for Ferrero dates back to the early 1980s when Morrison was photographer and picture editor for Paul Hamlyn in Sydney.

Bob Mossel, pilot and adventurer

Ferrero was fortunate to find such an experienced pilot whose knowledge of Australia was complemented by a working knowledge of aerial photography. Bob Mossel's meticulous records proved invaluable in researching dates and locations for this book.

David Parer, wildlife photographer and filmmaker

David Parer and his wife, Elizabeth Parer-Cook, have worked for the ABC Natural History Unit for more than 25 years. Their credits include *Wolves of the Sea* (1993) and *The Dragons of the Galapagos* (1998). David Parer's tribute on page viii is a personal and professional account of a highly regarded friend and colleague.

The publisher also wishes to thank Anne Ferrero for her interest and encouragement.

Viking
Penguin Books Australia Ltd
487 Maroondah Highway, PO Box 257
Ringwood, Victoria 3134, Australia
Penguin Books Ltd
Harmondsworth, Middlesex, England
Penguin Putnam Inc.
375 Hudson Street, New York, New York 10014, USA
Penguin Books Canada Limited
10 Alcorn Avenue, Toronto, Ontario, Canada M4V 3B2
Penguin Books (N.Z.) Ltd
Cnr Rosedale and Airborne Roads, Albany, Auckland, New Zealand
Penguin Books (South Africa) (Pty) Ltd
5 Watkins Street, Denver Ext 4, 2094, South Africa
Penguin Books India (P) Ltd, 11, Community Centre, Panchsheel Park
New Delhi 110 017, India

First published by Penguin Books Australia Ltd, 2001

10 9 8 7 6 5 4 3 2 1

Cover and internal design: Tony Palmer, Penguin Design Studio
Project editor: Heidi Marfurt
Research and editorial assistance: Susan McLeish
Production controller: Sue Van Velsen
Pre-press: Splitting Image Colour Studio Pty Ltd, Blackburn, Victoria
Printed in China by Midas Printing (Asia) Ltd

National Library of Australia
Cataloguing-in-Publication data

Ferrero, Jean-Paul, 1950–2000
    A remarkable eye: the Australian photographs of Jean-Paul Ferrero.

    ISBN 0 670 91193 3.

    1. Ferrero, Jean-Paul, 1950–2000. 2. Photography – Australia.
    3. Landscape photography – Australia. 4. Wildlife photography – Australia.
    5. Aerial photography – Australia. 6. Australia – Pictorial works. I. Title.

779/.092